KV-638-819

First published by Walker Books Ltd in
Big Bad Pig (1985), *Blow Me Down!* (1985),
Fee Fi Fo Fum (1985), *Help!* (1985), *Happy Worm* (1986),
Make a Face (1985) and *Tell Us a Story* (1986)

This edition published 1995

2 4 6 8 10 9 7 5 3 1

Text © 1985, 1986 Allan Ahlberg
Illustration © 1985, 1986 Colin McNaughton

This book has been typeset in ITC Garamond Light.

Printed in Belgium

British Library Cataloguing in Publication Data
A catalogue record for this book is
available from the British Library.
ISBN 0-7445-3737-1

WHO STOLE THE PIE?

Allan Ahlberg + Colin McNaughton

WALKER BOOKS
AND SUBSIDIARIES
LONDON • BOSTON • SYDNEY

three little pigs and a big bad wolf

three big pigs and a big bad wolf

three little wolves and a big bad pig

three little bad pigs and a big wolf

three little pigs and

a big good wolf

TABLE + CHAIR

table + chair + boy + girl +

knife + fork + spoon + plate

+ sandwich + cake + jelly

+ drink + hat + cracker =

party

THE PIE

Who made the pie?

I did!

Who stole the pie?

He did!

Who looked for the pie?

Who found the pie? Who ate the pie?

Who washed up?

Me!

CAT + FISH

pig + dinner = big pig

cow + grass = milk

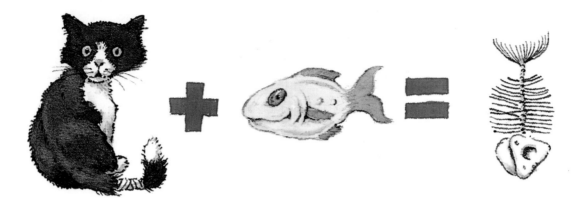

cat　+　fish　=　bones

BLOW ME DOWN!

"Blow me down!" says Burglar Bert. "Someone's pinched my football shirt."

"Blow me down!" says Burglar Paul. "Someone's pinched my bat and ball."

A catastrophe!

"Blow me down!" says Burglar Pat. "Someone's pinched my pussy cat."

"Blow me down!" says Burglar Jake. "Someone's pinched my birthday cake."

Crumbs!

Miaow!

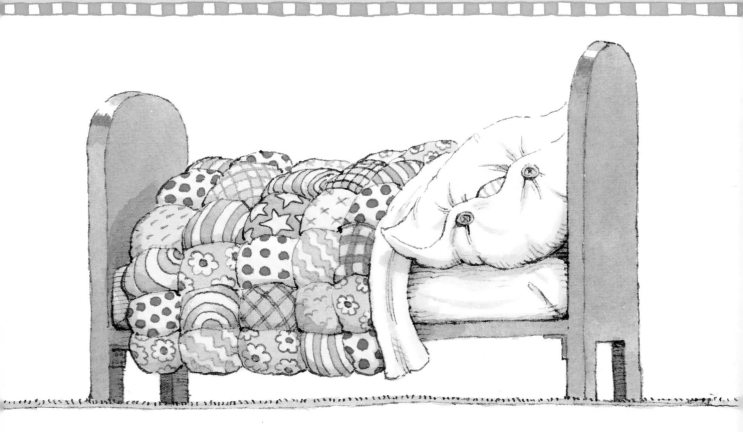

"Blow me down!"
says Burglar Freddy.
"Someone's pinched
my bedtime teddy."

MAKE A CASTLE

bucket   spade   flag   sand

make a castle

spade

flag

bucket

sand

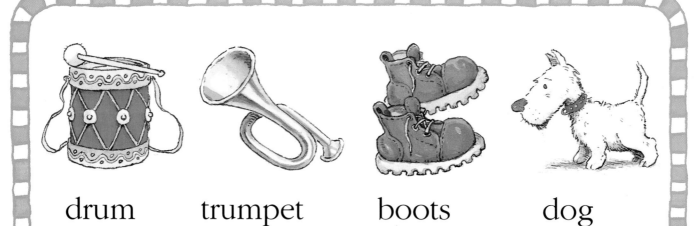

drum   trumpet   boots   dog

make a noise

trumpet

toot!

drum

boom!

bark!

boots

dog

bang!

bread

bananas

jam

cheese

fish

grapes

sausages

beans

make a ...

bread

cheese

jam

fish

beans

sausages

grapes

bananas

sandwich

The Pig

Two little boys climbed up to bed.

"Tell us a story, Dad,"
they said.

"Right!" said Dad.
"There was once a pig
who ate too much
and got so big
he couldn't sit down,
he couldn't bend…

Right!

So he ate standing up and got bigger –
The End!"

The Cat

"That story's
no good, Dad,"
the little boys said.
"Tell us a better one instead."

"Right!" said Dad. "There was once a cat
who ate too much
and got so fat
and got so fat
he split his fur
which he had
to mend

Right!

with a sewing machine and a zip –
The End!"

The Horse

"That story's
too mad, Dad,"

the little
boys said.

"Tell us another
one instead."

"Right!" said Dad. "There was once a horse who ate too much and died, of course – The End."

The Cow

"That story's too sad, Dad,"
the little boys said.
"Tell us a happier one instead."

Right…

"Right…" said Dad.

"There was once a cow

who ate so much that even now

she fills two fields

and blocks a road,

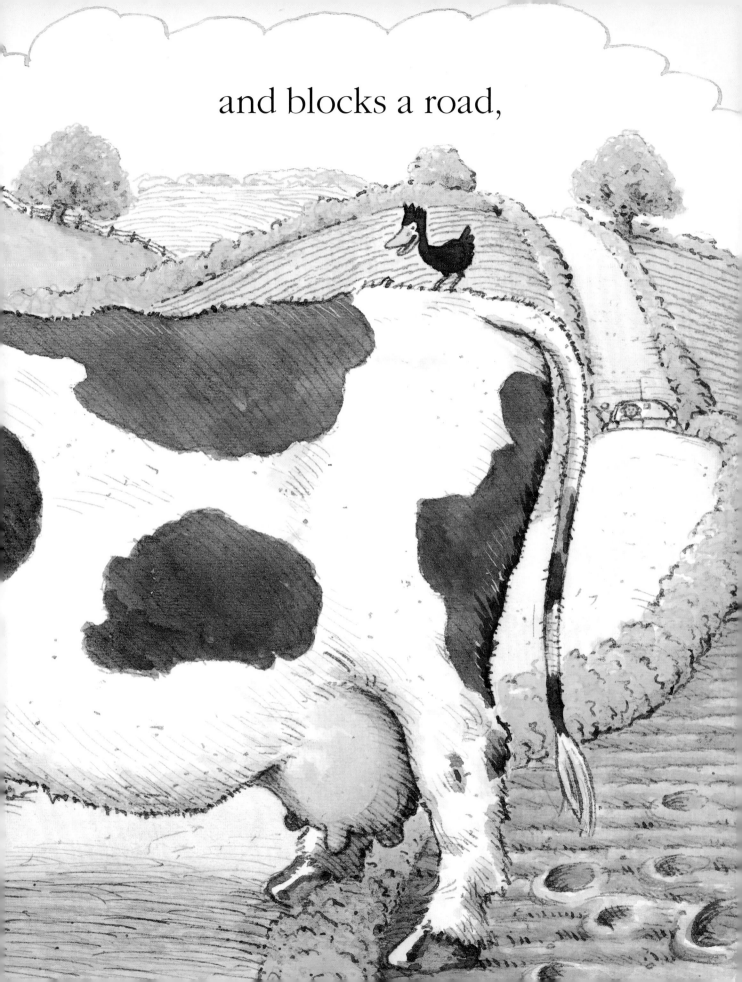

and when they milk her
she has to be towed!

She wins gold cups
and medals too,
for the creamiest milk
and the *loudest* moo!"

Moo!

"Now that's the end,"
said Dad. "No more."
And he shut his eyes
and began to snore.

Then the two little boys climbed out of bed
and crept downstairs…

to their Mum instead.

The End

the end